This book belongs to

. . . .

For Lulu, Eileen, Adi and Russell — T.M.
To my aita — E.O.

First published in Great Britain in 2006 by Andersen Press Ltd., 20 Vauxhall Bridge Road, London SW1V 2SA.
This paperback edition first published in 2017 by Andersen Press Ltd.
Text copyright © Tom MacRae, 2006. Illustration copyright © Elena Odriozola, 2006.
Text and cover design by David Mackintosh.
The rights of Tom MacRae and Elena Odriozola to be identified as the author and illustrator
of this work have been asserted by them in accordance with the Copyright, Designs and Patents Act, 1988.
All rights reserved. Colour separated in Switzerland by Photolitho AG, Zürich.
Printed and bound in China.

10   9   8   7   6   5   4   3   2   1

British Library Cataloguing in Publication Data available.

ISBN 978 1 84270 573 5

The
Opposite

By Tom MacRae

Illustrated by Elena Odriozola

Andersen Press

When Nate woke up one morning,
The Opposite was standing on
his ceiling, staring down at him.

"You can't stand on the ceiling,"
said Nate. "Get down!"

But The Opposite
happened, and it stayed
where it was.

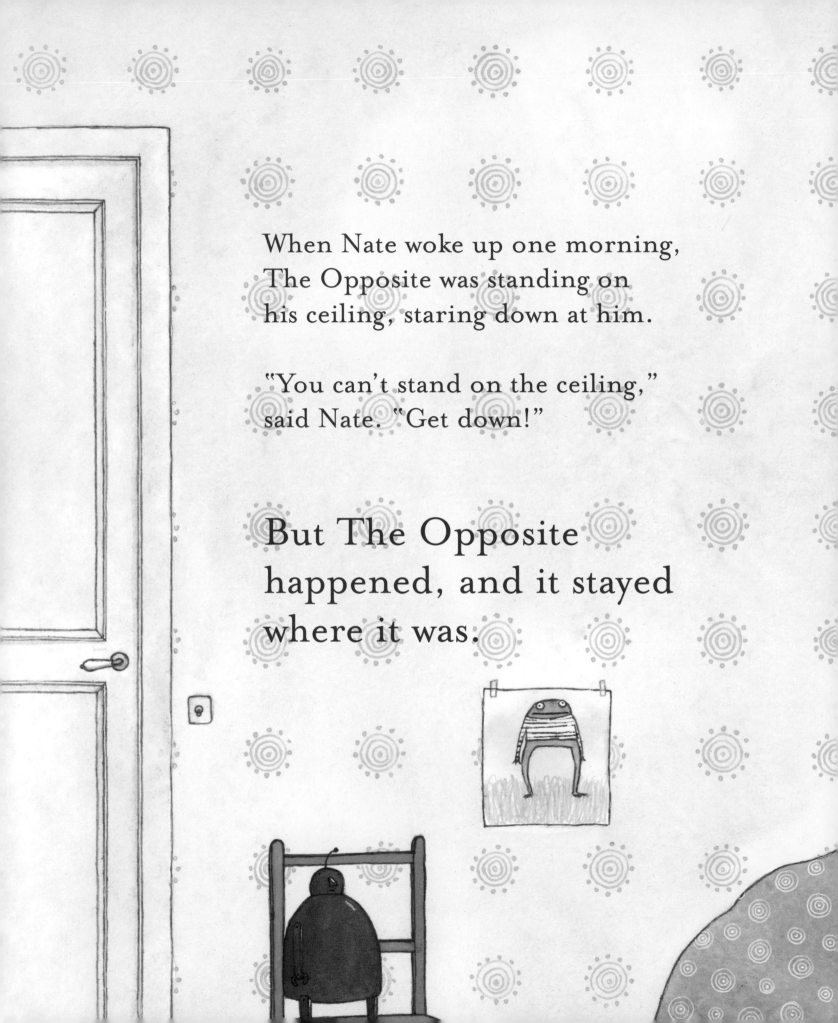

"Dad!" cried Nate. "There's an Opposite on my ceiling!"

"Where?" said Nate's dad, poking his head round the door.

"*There!*" said Nate, pointing upwards.

But The Opposite had already happened, and it wasn't there any more.

"Come on, Nate," said Nate's dad.
"You don't usually make up stories
to stay in bed."

Nate came downstairs to start his
breakfast. His mum poured out
a bowlful of cornflakes. "You can
do the milk yourself," she said.
Nate always did his own milk.
It was one of the things he
was best at.

Nate took the milk in both
hands and gently poured it
over the cereal.

But then
The Opposite
happened…

...instead of the milk pouring down, it poured UP, splashing all over the ceiling, then dripping down again all over the tablecloth. The Opposite grinned in the corner.

"Oh, Nate!" said Nate's mum. "Look what you've done!"

"It wasn't me!" cried Nate. "It was
The Opposite over there!" And Nate pointed
at the corner. But The Opposite had already
happened, and it wasn't there any more.

"Come on, Nate!"
said Nate's mum.
"You're not usually
so clumsy."

Nate walked into school and got ready
for the first lesson. Nate's teacher asked
the children to paint a picture of their
favourite animal. Nate decided to paint
an elephant. He took out his paint and
paper and brush, and made a start.

But then The Opposite happened.
Instead of the paint going on the paper,
it went on Nate's head.

Then on the floor.

Then on the walls.

Then on his teacher.

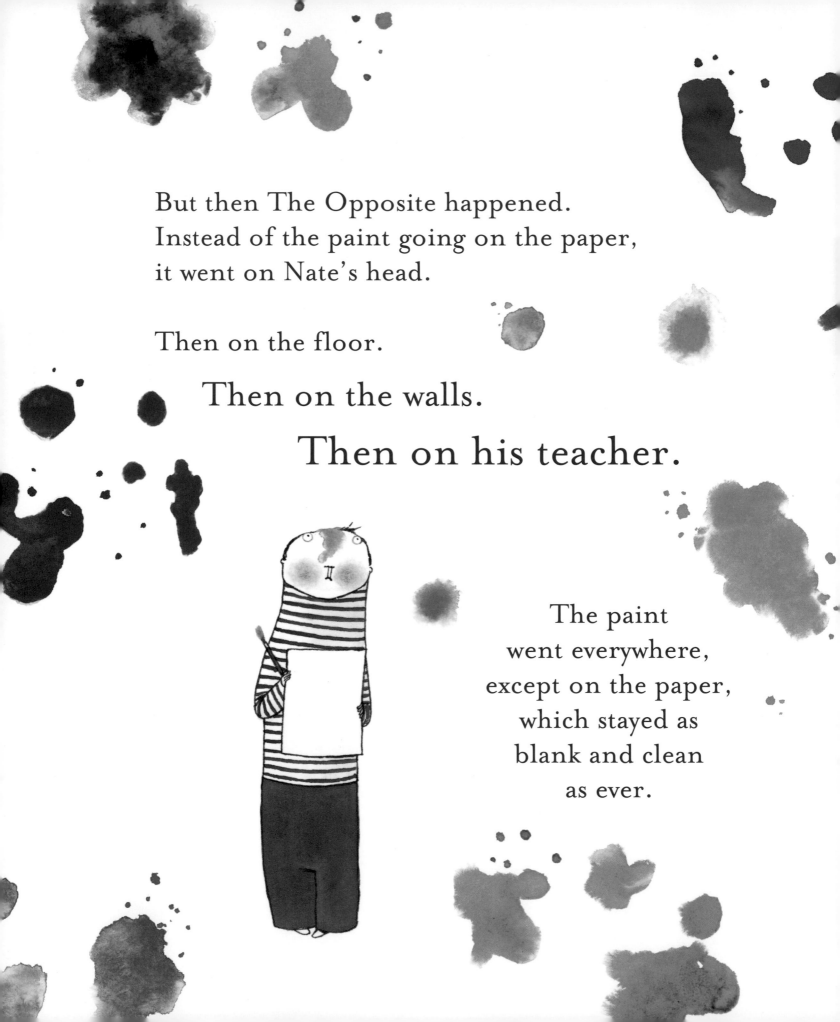

The paint
went everywhere,
except on the paper,
which stayed as
blank and clean
as ever.

The Opposite giggled from under the teacher's desk, right by the teacher's legs.

"Oh, Nate!" said Nate's teacher. "You're not usually so messy."

"It wasn't me!" cried Nate. "It was The Opposite under there!" And Nate pointed at the teacher's desk.

But The Opposite
had already happened,
and it wasn't there
any more.

Nate stopped, and thought for
a moment. Then he had an idea.
Slowly, he pointed at the empty
space in front of him.

"I mean to say," said Nate,
"that there ISN'T an Opposite
standing right in front
of my finger."

But then
The Opposite
happened.

Suddenly,
The Opposite
WAS standing
right in front
of Nate.

It blinked with
surprise,

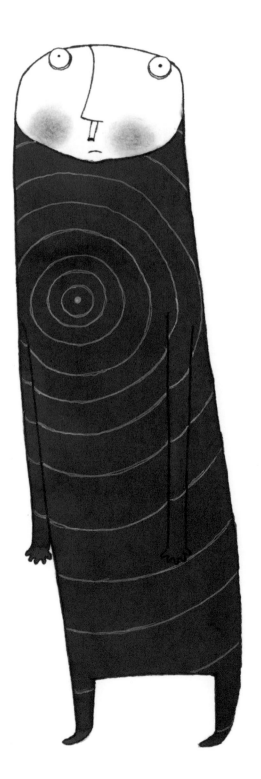

and
looked
a little
worried.

"I mean to say," said Nate. "That the work I have done today is messy and untidy."

But then The Opposite happened.

The Opposite bared its teeth, but it was too late. Nate's painting was now as tidy and perfect as you please.

"And," said Nate, smiling, "I mean to say that I have SO enjoyed having The Opposite with me today and I DO hope it will stay around for ever and ever and EVER!"

But then The Opposite happened.

...and a **hiss,**

The Opposite
disappeared
in a puff of
green and
yellow
smoke.

With a *shriek...*

And that was that. Very quickly,
Nate's teacher and the rest of Nate's
class persuaded themselves that they
had never seen The Opposite and
none of it had ever happened.

But Nate knew what had happened,
and now you do too. And if you
ever meet an Opposite, you will
know how to deal with it.

The next morning, when Nate woke up,
The Opposite was standing on his
ceiling, staring down at him.

"Oh good" said Nate. "I hope this story goes on for ever and EVER...

THE END!"

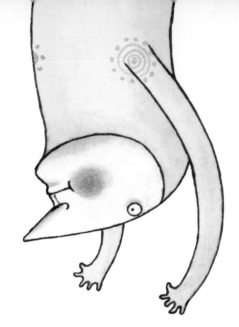